FABRIC AND STUFFING

SCISSORS AND MARKER

STRAIGHT PINS

THREAD AND NEEDLE

YARN IS OPTIONAL

1999

NOV

Nathan's Doll

WHAT YOU WILL NEED:
1/3 yard of fabric (any type or color will work)
Straight pins
Scissors
Needle and thread or sewing machine
(try to choose thread that is the same color as
the fabric you are using)
Stuffing (you can use fabric scraps, cotton, or
even old nylon stockings)
Colored markers or crayons
Yarn (optional)

INSTRUCTIONS:
Remember, don't be afraid to ask for help if you need it!

Trace or photocopy the figure pattern and cut out along the solid lines.

Fold fabric in half. Lay pattern on top and pin together, using straight pins. Cut out the two pattern pieces.

Using the needle and thread (you may also use a sewing machine, but be sure to ask an adult for help), sew the two pieces together, leaving a 1/4" seam all around. DO NOT stitch between dots at top of head.

Turn the sewn parts inside out. Stuff with stuffing through the head opening, then stitch the opening closed between the two dots.

Cut material at top of head into strips to make hair. Or, if you'd prefer, sew on strands of yarn.

Draw in eyes, nose, mouth, and any other decorations with markers or crayons.

by **Sonia Levitin** • Illustrated by **Cat Bowman Smith**

Taking Charge

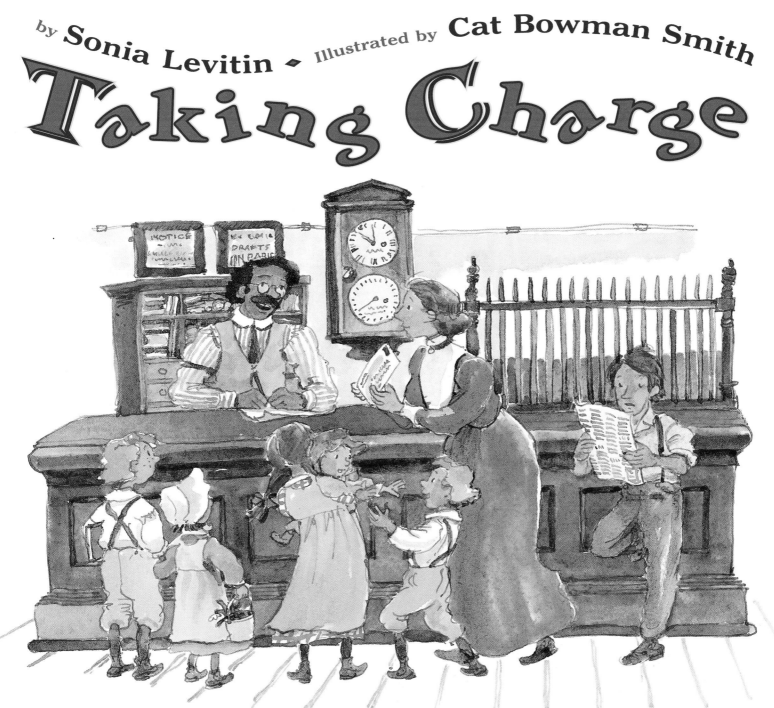

Orchard Books • New York

To the real Baby Nathan and
his proud grandma, Rita, with love
—S.L.

To Gabriel and Robert
—C.B.S.

Text copyright © 1999 by Sonia Levitin
Illustrations copyright © 1999 by Cat Bowman Smith

Orchard Books, A Grolier Company
95 Madison Avenue, New York, NY 10016

Manufactured in the United States of America
Printed and bound by Phoenix Color Corp.
Book design by Zara Design
The text of this book is set in 16 point Gloucester Old Style MT.
The illustrations are watercolor.

10 9 8 7 6 5 4 3 2 1

Library of Congress Cataloging-in-Publication Data
Levitin, Sonia, date.
Taking charge / by Sonia Levitin ;
illustrated by Cat Bowman Smith.
p.   cm. Sequel to: Boom town.
Summary: When her mother has to leave home suddenly, Amanda
learns how demanding it is to run a household and care for a baby.
ISBN 0-531-30149-4 (trade : alk. paper).
ISBN 0-531-33149-0 (lib. bdg. : alk. paper)
[1. Babies—Fiction. 2. Frontier and pioneer life—Fiction.]
I. Smith, Cat Bowman, ill.   II. Title.
PZ7.L58Tak   1999   [Fic]—dc21   98-36623

Dear Daughter,
I had a bit of a fall
and will be laid up. a
while. It would sure
pleasure me if you
could come and visit.
Hope your husband and
young 'ums are fine.
I am likewise, except I
can't walk or do much
around the house.
Your loving Ma

Mama got a letter from her ma in Missouri. Grandma had had an accident.

Mama wanted to go tend her right away. "But how can I leave all you young 'uns?" she said. Amanda saw her starting to think. "I could take Betsy along," Mama said, "but what about Baby Nathan? I'd be worn out carrying him all over creation and taking care of my ma too."

"I can watch Baby Nathan," said Amanda. "He's no trouble."

Mama looked doubtful. "You'd have to cook for Pa and your brothers and do all my chores. Of course, it's summer, and you don't have school. . . ."

"Let me do it, Mama," Amanda begged. "Let me take charge for a while."

Mama smiled and said, "I guess it's okay, Amanda. Baby Nathan isn't walking yet. He'll stay right where you put him."

Mama talked to Pa, and it was settled.

The next morning everyone took Mama and Betsy to the station. Brothers Billy, Joe, and Ted ran ahead. Amanda came last, with Baby Nathan in her arms. Baby Nathan was getting heavy. At the station she set him down in the shade.

Billy, Joe, and Ted whooped and hollered when the stage came in. Betsy laughed and waved good-bye. Mama gave Amanda a big kiss. "I know you can manage," said Mama, "but don't be afraid to ask for help when you need it."

"Bye, Mama. Don't worry," said Amanda. "Everything will be fine."

"Giddyap!" yelled the driver, and the horses took off in a cloud of dust.
Amanda looked around for Baby Nathan. "Pa, have you got Nathan?"
"I sure don't," said Pa. "I'll look around back. Get Billy, Joe, and Ted to help."

But the boys were running off to buy penny candy. Besides, Amanda was the one in charge. She heard hollering. She ran inside the station house. There was Baby Nathan on the stationmaster's desk. Nathan's fat little fingers clicked away, *rattle, tattle, tum.*

"Get that baby away from my brand-new telegraph machine!" shouted the stationmaster.

"Baby Nathan!" cried Amanda, and she leaned over to scoop him up. But Baby Nathan scrambled down from the desk and *walked* away, fast.

Amanda ran and caught him in her arms. She panted. "How come you'd start walking now, just when Mama's left?"

"Mum-mum," said Baby Nathan.

Home again, Amanda laid Baby Nathan down for a nap, while Billy, Joe, and Ted did their chores and Pa tended the bakery.

Amanda made the beds and swept the floor. She dusted chairs and set the table. Mama had left some cold meat for supper. Biscuits would be good, Amanda thought, biscuits and butter. Usually she and Mama took turns at the butter churn. Now Amanda sat pumping and churning alone. Her head dropped down, and before she knew it, she was asleep. Amanda awoke to a yell and a gurgle.

"Mum-mum!"

Amanda jumped up. The butter churn swayed. Inside was Baby Nathan, dripping and creamy. Amanda pulled him out. He clung to her and cried. It took forever to get Baby Nathan clean again, and even longer to clean the floor. Then it was suppertime.

Amanda brought out the meat, some withered tomatoes, and a cold potato or two.
"What's this?" yelled the boys. "You said you could cook, Amanda!"
"You could help instead of complaining," said Pa.
"I don't need any help," said Amanda. "Not from those boys."

By Monday there was washing to do. It took Amanda nearly all day, fetching the water, heating it up, scrubbing the clothes on a board, rinsing them out, and hanging them up to dry.

Miss Millie, their neighbor, came along. "Looks like you could use some help, Amanda," she said.

"No thanks, Miss Millie. I'm doing just fine," said Amanda.

All day Baby Nathan followed along at Amanda's feet. Suddenly Amanda heard a splash and a gurgle. She ran to the washtub. Inside, Papa's red long johns were mixing it up with Billy's green socks, Ted's blue pants, and Joe's yellow shirt. Amanda's pink dress and Mama's best white apron floated on top.

"Baby Nathan!" Amanda cried. "You mixed all the colors!" She pulled him away, but it was too late.

The boys and Pa came trooping in. "What's for supper, Amanda? Did you make those biscuits yet?"

"Not yet," said Amanda, glaring. She served up a pot of beans that Mama had left for them. Billy, Joe, Ted, and Pa ate the beans without a word. Baby Nathan ate the beans and belched. Too late Amanda realized that beans and babies don't go together.

Miss Camilla sent for Amanda one day. "We're having a quilting bee at my house," she said. "All the ladies are coming. Some are bringing their babies. You could bring Baby Nathan and spend the day."

Amanda was glad to go. She took her basket of sewing scraps and bundled up Baby Nathan. Snug in Miss Camilla's house, Amanda sat with the ladies, stitching and chatting, sipping tea and eating dainty finger sandwiches.

Soon all the patches were sewn and the backing was done. "It's time to put the quilt together," Miss Camilla said. She looked on the table. She looked on the floor. She opened the cupboard door. "Where is the quilt?" she said.

From outside came a happy squeal and a shout. "Mum-mum!"
Out in the little pen where the pigs lived sat Baby Nathan all mired in the mud. Mama pig had the quilt tucked around her.

"Baby Nathan!" screamed Amanda. "Oh, Miss Camilla, I'm sorry as can be!" Miss Camilla tried to smile, but her mouth was held tight as she whispered, "It's all right."

Supper that night was bread and milk. "And nobody better complain!" grumbled Amanda.
Billy, Joe, and Ted rolled their eyes and puckered their faces. "You might ask Miss Camilla for
some cooking tips," Pa said lightly.

"Thanks, Pa," said Amanda, "but I can manage."

Pa said, "I've got to deliver some pies to the railroad crew. I'll stop in the city for supplies.
Amanda, I need you to go to the bank and bring back some cash."

Next morning Amanda set out, with Baby Nathan along. At the bank Mr. Hooper tipped his hat and went to count out some coins. They talked for a time, and Amanda felt fine until she saw that Baby Nathan was gone.

"Baby Nathan! Baby Nathan, where are you?"

Mr. Hooper called the teller and the guard. Everyone searched for Baby Nathan. Then Amanda saw the big steel safe. It was shut tight. Amanda pressed her ear to the door. She heard a faint sound. "Mum-mum."

Mr. Hooper came running. He opened the outer door with a combination. A smaller door stood behind it, locked. Mr. Hooper twisted his hat in his hands. "The key is gone," he said. "Baby Nathan must have it with him."

"We've got to get help," wailed Amanda. "Send for the blacksmith, please!"

Mr. Hooper called the blacksmith. He came with his crowbar and hammer. At last he broke through. Amanda looked inside. There sat Baby Nathan playing with a pile of gold coins.

Later, for supper, Amanda cracked open some eggs and left them standing in a bowl while she went to fetch kindling. When she got back, Baby Nathan had his fingers in the eggs, along with a few other things he had found.

"Baby Nathan!" Amanda screamed. "You wrecked my eggs!"

Amanda looked in the cooler box. All the leftovers were gone.

"Too late to make anything else," she said. "I'll just have to fry all this together."

Billy, Joe, Ted, and Pa smacked their lips. "Delicious, Amanda," they said. Amanda started to say that Baby Nathan helped. But she didn't.

Next morning Pa gathered up pies and supplies, and went on the road. "I'll be back in a day or two," he said. "If you need help, Amanda, just ask for it."

Amanda looked at Baby Nathan, sitting on the floor, and figured out a plan. She picked him up and took off for town. First she stopped at Miss Camilla's.

Miss Camilla was glad to help.

Then she went to Cowboy Charlie's. He was glad to lend a hand.

Finally Amanda knocked at Miss Millie's door and asked for her help too.

Miss Millie smiled and asked Amanda in. She and Amanda sat down at the table. They drew and cut, they stuffed and stitched while Baby Nathan watched. Soon they had made two dolls for Baby Nathan—a boy doll and a horse with real horsehair.

"Here you go, Nathan," said Amanda, handing him the dolls. "That ought to keep you busy."

Sure enough, Baby Nathan played with his toys the rest of the day, staying right by Amanda while she washed the dishes and ironed some clothes, weeded a patch and picked some corn, sewed a hem and fixed supper for everyone. Eggs for dinner were a treat, with corn and onions, all chopped together. The boys were happy, and so was Amanda. "It's easy being in charge," she said. But that evening she was so tired she fell asleep in her chair, with Baby Nathan on her lap.

In darkness Amanda woke up. The candles had burned out. Baby Nathan was gone!
Amanda ran through the rooms. She looked outside, fearing wolves and robbers. Amanda
ran through the town. At Cowboy Charlie's stable she saw a small person sitting on the fence.
"Baby Nathan, what are you doing?" Amanda cried.

"Mum-mum," shouted Baby Nathan.

Then Amanda smelled the smoke. She saw the flames. She grabbed Baby Nathan and ran to the schoolhouse as fast as she could. "Help!" she shouted as she rang the schoolhouse bell. "Cowboy Charlie's stable is on fire! Help!"

Help!

Billy, Joe, and Ted came running with buckets and shovels.
Soon the whole town was awake, putting out the fire.

Everyone praised Amanda for saving the town.
"Thank you," said Amanda. "But I
had help." She smiled at her brothers.
Everyone cheered. Baby Nathan clapped
his hands.

When Mama got back, they all went to meet her. Amanda carried Baby Nathan. It was a hot day, so she set him down in the shade. "Mum-mum!" Baby Nathan shouted as Mama got down from the stage. Mama ran to pick him up.

"Baby Nathan," she said, "I see you're not walking yet. Well, at least you didn't give your sister any trouble."

Amanda only smiled. Later she'd tell Mama all about it. Right now she was just glad to have Mama back home.

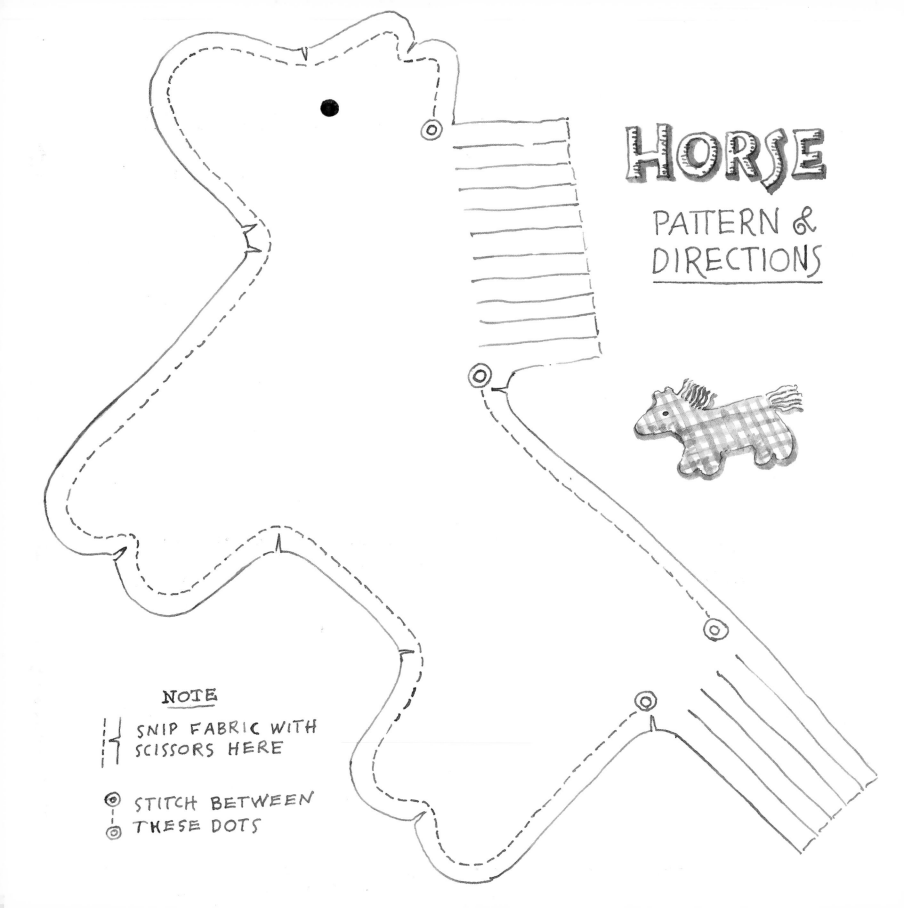

HORSE

PATTERN & DIRECTIONS

NOTE

Snip fabric with scissors here

Stitch between these dots